Check out the  Y0-BZY-789
▼ STECK-VAUGHN Mysteries!

Bases are loaded . . . in more ways than one.
Find out why in
STOLEN BASES

Who's at the screen of the crime?
Get the answer in
MODEM MENACE

Here's a job that will really haunt you.
Check out
GRAVE DISCOVERY

It's time to face the music! Take a look at
SEE NO EVIL

Who's *really* behind the wall?
See for yourself in
A BONE TO PICK

Who's calling? Get the answer, read
PLEASE CALL BACK!

Somebody's inside . . . but nobody should be.
See who in
ANYBODY HOME?

Someone's planning an *un*welcome.
Find out more in
HOME, CREEPY, HOME

Shop . . . until you drop!
Read all about it in
BUYING TROUBLE

ISBN 0-8114-9302-4

Copyright ©1995 Steck-Vaughn Company. All rights reserved. No part of the
material protected by this copyright may be reproduced or utilized in any form
or by any means, electronic or mechanical, including photocopying, recording,
or by any information storage and retrieval system, without permission in
writing from the copyright owner. Requests for permission to make copies of
any part of the work should be mailed to: Copyright Permissions, Steck-Vaughn
Company, P.O. Box 26015, Austin, TX 78755. Printed in the United States of
America.

1 2 3 4 5 6 7 8 9 98 97 96 95 94

Produced by Mega-Books of New York, Inc.
Design and Art Direction by Michaelis/Carpelis Design Assoc.

Cover illustration: Ken Spencer

TERROR TRAIL

by Alex Simmons

interior illustrations by
Don Morrison

DESERT SANDS UNIFIED SCHOOL DISTRICT

PALM DESERT
MIDDLE
LIBRARY

No. 95-001
Date APR 25 '95

INDIO, CALIFORNIA

STECK-VAUGHN
COMPANY

Chapter · 1

"I can't believe you aren't thrilled by all this," said Mrs. Ashby.

"I don't get excited about trees, Mom," grumbled fifteen-year-old Mark Ashby. "Squirrels like trees. I like VCRs, stacks of tapes, and large pizzas with everything."

"And I'd like a hot shower," added Carla, Mark's thirteen-year-old sister.

The Ashbys were on a horseback riding tour through the Canadian Rocky Mountains. Although Mark and Carla argued a lot, they agreed on one thing: The great outdoors wasn't that great.

The tour guides, Paul Travers and Shirley Cloud, were pretty friendly.

Their boss, Mr. Cariou, had come along, too. But he was always riding off far ahead of everyone else. Right now, in fact, no one knew where he was.

The rest of the group was on a ridge overlooking a large, pine-green valley. Down below, a paved road curved and twisted down along the mountain. Below that, Mark and Carla could see a winding river and a small lake.

"We'll camp by the river tonight," Paul told the group. "And then tomorrow . . ."

"We're sleeping outdoors *again*?" Mark mumbled. He was not pleased.

The group kept riding until they reached a point where the trail crossed the paved road. Shirley gave a sign to stop. A shiny milk tanker drove by slowly. The two men in the tanker waved.

"Maybe I could hitch a ride back to the city," Mark suggested.

"Not without me," Carla warned him.

Paul chuckled. "Hey, come on, kids. Where's your sense of adventure?" he asked.

Carla frowned. "At the mall," she said.

Farther down the mountain they passed a paint factory. A truck was parked in front.

"What is a paint factory doing way out here?" Carla asked.

"This was once a big logging area," Shirley explained. "We'll pass the old, abandoned logging camp in a couple of miles."

7

"So, what's that got to do with paint?" asked Mark.

"The loggers planned to build a town," Shirley continued. "They put up some houses. A paint factory and a few other companies moved in. But the logging business failed. Most of the people moved away. The paint factory had too much money invested to move. So, they stayed."

An hour later, the group rode past the abandoned logging camp. Three wooden buildings stood near a steep drop. Two of the buildings looked like small barns.

Carla noticed thick tire tracks in front of one building. "That one must have been the garage," she thought.

The third building was larger. It had been the sawmill. An old wooden slide was attached to one side. It ran all the way down the mountain at a very steep angle. The slide ended ten feet above a river at the foot of the mountain.

"That slide looks like a ski jump," Mark said.

"Yeah, but the building looks haunted," whispered Carla.

An hour later, the tired group finally reached the campsite. Mr. Cariou was already there. He had picked out a clearing and built a fire.

"Take your horses over to the river for a drink," ordered Mr. Cariou. "But don't let them drink too much."

"Why?" Carla asked him.

"It's not good for them. That's why." The tour boss walked away before Carla could say another word.

"He is major rude," Carla said, turning to Mark.

Mark grinned. "So are you, sometimes," he teased, pretending to punch her.

Carla ignored him. And when the others led their horses back to camp, Carla stayed behind. She walked her horse away from the river and down to the lake's edge.

"You should know when you've had enough," Carla told the horse. The animal began drinking again. "Drink all you want," she added.

That night, Mark and Carla crawled into their tent and stared out the front flap. The lake looked like a sheet of dark glass. All around them they heard hoots, howls, snaps, scratches, and hisses.

Their mother had forced them to share a tent. She said it would help them learn to get along. So far, Mrs. Ashby's plan wasn't working very well.

"Don't wake me up like you did last night," Carla warned Mark.

"I won't," Mark snapped back. "Not even if I see something creepy crawl into your sleeping bag."

Carla was about to hit him when they heard a wild, screaming whine.

Chapter · 2

Carla and Mark grabbed their flashlights and scrambled out of the tent. They saw Shirley struggling with one of the horses. The horse was foaming and going wild.

Paul jumped in front of the horse and waved his hands, trying to calm it down. Then, all of a sudden, the horse fell to the ground. It was breathing hard. Its whole body was heaving.

"What's wrong with it?" Mark asked as he and Carla inched closer.

Shirley began carefully examining the horse. She looked very worried.

"I think it's been poisoned," she said.

After a few minutes, Shirley started

toward the other horses. "I'll check all the horses. In the morning we'll have to look around for signs of poisonous berries or plants," she told them.

Just then Mr. Cariou came running into the camp. He was carrying a flashlight and his pant legs were wet.

"I took a walk," he explained. "I heard the noise, but it took me some time to get back here."

Paul told his boss what had happened to the horse.

"Mr. Cariou doesn't seem too surprised by the news," Carla whispered to Mark.

Suddenly Mr. Cariou turned toward Carla. "This is your horse," he said, staring at her.

Carla's eyes widened in surprise. In all the excitement, she hadn't recognized her horse.

Mr. Cariou continued. "Did you feed it something that would . . ."

"My sister didn't poison your horse!"

Mark interrupted angrily.

Carla suddenly burst into tears and ran toward the lake. Mark quickly took off after her.

"It *is* my fault," Carla sobbed. "I let the horse drink too much water. That's why it's sick."

"Shirley said poisoned, not sick," Mark reminded her.

"Still, it might be my fault," Carla said. She wiped the tears from her face. "So I'm going to take a look around."

Mark turned to Carla. "I'm going with you," he said. Carla looked surprised.

Mark shrugged. "Well, I *am* your big brother," he explained. "Besides, there's nothing else to do around here."

A few moments later they were standing at the edge of the lake.

"This is where I watered my horse," Carla told Mark. She moved her flashlight beam along the ground.

"Hey, check this out!" Carla cried. She pointed to some markings on the

ground. "Doesn't it look like some giant
snake crawled along here?" she asked.

"Well, something dragged along the
ground," Mark agreed.

Carla and Mark stared at each other for a second. Then they started off, following the trail of markings. A few feet into the woods, the trail ended by a pool of reddish-green liquid.

"What is this stuff?" Mark asked.

"I don't know," answered Carla. "But look at this." The bodies of several small animals were lying nearby. Mark and Carla moved closer toward them.

"Are they . . ." Carla began.

"Yeah," Mark said quickly. "I wonder if they were poisoned, too."

"Hey, look at this," Carla called out suddenly. She was pointing to a set of tire tracks.

"These are from a big truck," Mark said. "What would a big truck be doing up here?" he wondered out loud.

"Making a secret delivery," Carla said excitedly. "And this red-green stuff probably oozed out of the truck when it stopped."

"That's it!" Mark shouted. "Someone

is dumping poison into the water. And the truck's hose made those snakelike markings on the ground."

Carla went back to the tire tracks. "Look! The tracks lead up the hill toward the old logging camp!" she cried.

Chapter · 3

Mark and Carla crouched down behind one of the logging camp buildings. "Explain to me again why we didn't go get Shirley or Paul," Carla whispered.

Mark sighed heavily. "Because we don't want to look like jerks," he explained. "If we find something, then we'll go for help. Come on."

Carla and Mark moved around to the front of one building.

Carla shined her flashlight on the ground. "We saw this building this morning," she said. "Here are those old tire tracks."

Mark stared at the ground. "That

doesn't make sense," he said. "Shirley said this place was abandoned. Rain would have washed away any old tracks. These tracks must be new. They look like they were made by a truck."

Carla gripped Mark's arm. "Like the truck at the paint factory?" she asked.

Mark shined his flashlight beam on the building's doors. They were locked. But through the cracks the light glittered off something inside.

Before they could get closer, Mark and Carla heard a strange sound. It was coming from the sawmill.

"Now do we go get help?" Carla whispered.

"In a minute," Mark said as they hurried across to the sawmill. They found an open side door and entered the building quietly.

The sawmill was a big room with a

high ceiling and large doors on one side. Except for an old rain barrel and a very long table, it was empty.

The table was where logs had been cut. It was still connected to the old, wooden log slide through a cut-out window.

Carla swallowed hard. "It's spooky in here. Let's go back outside," she said to Mark.

"Okay," Mark agreed, his voice trembling.

"It's too late," a voice crackled from the darkness. "You're not going back anywhere!"

Suddenly Mark and Carla heard a piercing, whining noise.

"That sounds like an electric saw!" Mark shouted.

"Time to cut the logs!" laughed the crackling voice. The whining noise grew louder and closer.

"Let's get out of here!" Carla screamed.

Mark grabbed the old rain barrel. He pushed it up onto the long table, near the window opening for the log slide.

"Jump in!" Mark yelled to Carla.

The sound of the electric saw drew closer. Carla leaped into the barrel and Mark pushed it out through the window. He jumped in just as the barrel began to slide down the chute.

The barrel picked up speed rapidly.

The old wooden log slide rocked and shook. Then the barrel shot out into space. Mark and Carla screamed as they dropped into the darkness.

Chapter · 4

The river was as cold as ice.

"Swim toward the shore!" Mark yelled to Carla.

"No kidding!" she gasped.

They swam as fast as they could. But the cold inched along their fingers and legs, making it harder and harder for them to move quickly.

Just when they thought they wouldn't make it, Carla and Mark felt the rocky ground below the water. They crawled onto the shore. Suddenly they were grabbed by strong, powerful hands.

Mark looked up. It was Mr. Cariou. Mark struggled to break free.

"Easy does it, son," said a Royal

Canadian Mounted Police officer who had stepped up to help.

Mark shook his head clear. He saw his mother was already wrapping a jacket around Carla.

"Mr. Cariou found your footprints at the lake," Mrs. Ashby told Mark and Carla. "I was worried. Then we heard you screaming as you went down that slide. That was a very dangerous thing to do!" she scolded.

"We weren't playing, Mom!" Carla tried to explain. "We found some dead

animals and . . ."

"I know," Mr. Cariou interrupted. "I found them just before your horse got sick. So I started looking around the lake and the river. I even took samples of the water. The lake has been polluted with some kind of poison."

"So that's why your pant legs were wet," Carla said to Mr. Cariou.

"We thought the paint factory might be dumping chemicals into the lake," said the Mountie. "But we didn't know how. None of their trucks have been seen near the lake."

"I thought that too, so I've been spying on them," added Mr. Cariou.

Mark snapped his fingers. "Is that why you've been riding ahead of us, to check for clues?" he asked.

Mr. Cariou nodded. "Yeah, and that's why I asked you about what you fed the horse," he said to Carla. "I had to make sure it could only have been the water that made the horse sick."

"Well, whoever is doing the polluting is using a big truck," Carla said. She then told them about the tire tracks and the reddish-green liquid.

"The paint factory truck is small," said Mr. Cariou. "So who could it be?"

"I think I know!" Mark exclaimed. "Let's get to the sawmill, quick!"

They all piled into the police car. The Mountie put the car in gear and took off with tires screeching. Just as they rounded the turn near the logging camp, Mark shouted, "There they are!"

Headed straight for them was a milk tanker. Its large body shined in the

moonlight. In no time, the police car closed in on the truck.

The Mountie drew his gun and walked over to the truck. He motioned to the two men to get out.

"What's the problem, sir?" the driver asked nervously.

"I'll let you know after I check the contents of your truck," the Mountie told him.

Mark and Carla stared at the driver. They had heard his crackling voice

before—in the sawmill! They knew the Mountie had the right men.

Several hours later, the Mountie stopped by the campsite. Shirley was feeding the sick horse.

"How's the horse doing?" the Mountie asked her.

"I think it's going to be all right," answered Shirley.

The Mountie then told everyone how things had turned out.

"The two men we caught have been hauling milk to a dairy near here," he explained. "When they left the dairy, they would go by the paint factory and pick up a load of chemical waste."

Carla made a face. "In the same truck? Gross!" she groaned.

"They must have parked their truck in the old logging camp until it was dark," Mark said. "I'll bet that's what we saw glittering inside the building."

"You got it," the Mountie said grimly. "They dumped the waste into the lake at night. You two almost found them, so they tried to scare you off, using a chainsaw."

"What will happen to them?" Mark asked.

"The two men and the paint factory owner have been arrested," answered the Mountie. "They won't be seeing this view for some time. Not with the charges they face."

Carla and Mark turned around. The sun was rising over the mountains. Yellow and red rays of light sparkled in the river.

"Well, are you sorry you came?" Mrs. Ashby asked her children.

Mark and Carla gave each other a quick glance.

"Well, the city sure is nothing like this," admitted Mark.

"But I still could use a hot shower," Carla added.

"You sure could," Mark teased as Carla chased him around the camp.